LISTEN... LEARN... LOVE...
CLASSICAL MUSIC WITH

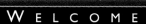

Dear Music Lover,

Why have we sent this extraordinary gift to you? We have found that most people enjoy classical music but never pursue it because they find the number of composers and styles of the music overwhelming. Giving you one of our *In Classical Mood* concerts to enjoy is simply the easiest way to show you how our music experts make learning and enjoying classical music easy. But don't take our word for it, take a look and listen to the Concert-in-a-Book we sent you today and decide for yourself.

Start with our CD featuring some of the most enduring overtures ever written. Then dive into our gorgeous hardcover Listener's Guide that takes you inside the music with riveting stories. The more you learn about classical music, the more you'll enjoy listening to it!

To enjoy more *In Classical Mood* Concerts, return your Concert Savings Voucher together with your Concert Admission Form today.

Enjoy!

Sincerely,

Arthur Fleming

Arthur Fleming
Editorial Director

In Classical Mood, 444 Liberty Avenue, Pittsburgh, PA 15222-1207. 1-800-834-2086

Great Overtures

Originally, the overture was created as a means to gain the attention of a restless audience. However, over the centuries, the operatic overture has blossomed into one of the world's best-loved musical forms. This volume of *In Classical Mood* features eleven of the greatest overtures, including Mozart's sublimely tuneful *Marriage of Figaro*, Wagner's dramatic *Mastersingers*, Beethoven's mournful masterpiece *Fidelio*, and Rossini's *William Tell*.

THE LISTENER'S GUIDE — WHAT THE SYMBOLS MEAN

THE COMPOSERS
Their lives... their loves.. their legacies...

THE MUSIC
Explanation... analysis... interpretation...

THE INSPIRATION
How works of genius came to be written

THE BACKGROUND
People, places, and events linked to the music

© MCMXCVI IMP AB   In Classical Mood™   IMP AB, produced under license by IMP Inc.   Printed in China.   US P 2201 12 006

Contents

– 2 –
Carmen: Prelude
GEORGES BIZET

– 4 –
Candide: Overture
LEONARD BERNSTEIN

– 6 –
La Traviata: Prelude
GIUSEPPE VERDI

– 8 –
Oberon: Overture
CARL MARIA VON WEBER

– 10 –
The Wasps: Overture
RALPH VAUGHAN WILLIAMS

– 13 –
The Marriage of Figaro: Overture
WOLFGANG AMADEUS MOZART

– 14 –
The Mastersingers of Nuremberg: Overture
RICHARD WAGNER

– 17 –
The Nutcracker: Miniature Overture
PYOTR TCHAIKOVSKY

– 19 –
Fidelio: Overture
LUDWIG VAN BEETHOVEN

– 22 –
The Yeomen of the Guard: Overture
SIR ARTHUR SULLIVAN

– 23 –
William Tell: Overture
GIOACHINO ROSSINI

GEORGES BIZET *1838–1875*

Carmen

PRELUDE

*C*armen is a wild Spanish gypsy girl who seduces a young soldier, Don José, then abandons him for the dashing *toreador* (bullfighter) Escamillo. In his despair, Don José stabs Carmen to death on the day of the bullfight. The prelude carries us straight to the heart of the action: A procession of bullfighters marching through the streets of Seville to the tune of Escamillo's famous "Toreador's Song." The music marvelously conveys the pageantry of the occasion, the proud swagger of Escamillo, and all the warmth, color, and romance of southern Spain.

WHY A PRELUDE?

By the 1870s, when Georges Bizet was working on *Carmen*, the operatic overture (a piece of music separate from the opera itself) was already rather old-fashioned. Most composers preferred to write a much shorter orchestral piece—a prelude—intended to set the scene and lead straight into the opera without a break. So, Bizet dispensed with an overture to *Carmen* and gave us this brief, but wonderfully vivid, prelude instead.

A BELATED SUCCESS

Bizet studied music at the Paris Conservatoire de Musique from age nine to age twenty. During that time he wrote the brilliant *Symphony in C,* at only seventeen, and won the coveted *Grand Prix de Rome* for composition at nineteen. Like all French composers of his time, Bizet desperately wanted to write successful operas. Instead, a succession of failures robbed him of his confidence and he died at the age of thirty-seven without enjoying any of the acclaim that his music has received.

OPENING NIGHT DISASTER

Carmen is perhaps the best-loved opera in the world, but it was not an instant success. At its premiere *(below)* in Paris on March 3, 1875, many in the audience were shocked by its stark realism: Carmen and her coworkers from a cigarette factory smoking on stage and the sordid stabbing at the end. The sheer dramatic power of the music also proved a little too much for those who had come to the theater simply to be entertained. Unfortunately, Bizet died of a heart attack three months later, just before his operatic masterpiece became a spectacular success.

KEY NOTES

"I must have a stage," Bizet once said. *"Without it, I am nothing."*

3

LEONARD BERNSTEIN *1918–1990*

Candide

OVERTURE

T he comic operetta *Candide* is based on the novel by 18th-century French writer Voltaire. Adhering closely to the story of the original novel, the operetta follows the adventures of Candide and his lover, Cunégonde, as they travel around the world, experiencing a shipwreck, an earthquake, and piracy on the way. At the end of their travels, they are forced to the conclusion that is better to make the best of reality than to strive for perfection, which is the moral of the tale. They buy a farm and settle down. This brilliant overture, bubbling over with tuneful laughter, foretells the operetta's happy end.

A PLAY ON WORDS

The American playwright Lillian Hellman first interested Leonard Bernstein in the novels of Voltaire *(left)*. She planned to adapt *Candide* as a play and asked him to write some incidental (accompanying) music for it. But when Bernstein read the book, he loved it so much that he asked for it to be turned into a musical stage show. The show was not a great hit, but the overture quickly became one of Bernstein's most popular pieces of music.

BIGGEST AND BRIGHTEST

The composer and conductor Leonard Bernstein is one of the biggest and brightest names in American music. He reached the pinnacle of his conducting career as director of the New York Philharmonic Orchestra. His performances, especially those of Mahler's dramatic symphonies, made him world-famous. As a composer, Bernstein was astonishingly versatile. His music ranges from the jazz-inspired scores he wrote for the hit stage and screen musicals *On the Town* and *West Side Story (right)* through the clever satire of *Candide*, to much more musically serious works such as his *Symphony No.2*, nicknamed *"The Age of Anxiety."* The supremely talented Bernstein was also a fine pianist and later became an influential teacher, witty and perceptive critic, and popular broadcaster.

Bernstein (left) *claimed that his greatest enemy was time and that he "never had quite enough" to do the things that he wanted to do.*

KEY NOTES

Bernstein also wrote the music for the classic 1954 movie On the Waterfront, starring Marlon Brando. It was his only full movie score.

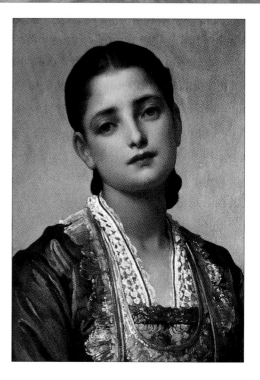

GIUSEPPE VERDI *1813–1901*

La Traviata

PRELUDE

T he scenario of *La Traviata* is based on a play by the French writer Alexandre Dumas, Junior called *La Dame aux Camélias* (the "Lady of the Camelias"). It is about a Parisian courtesan, Violetta, who leaves her lover, Alfredo, for the sake of his family's reputation. Without knowing her motives, Alfredo then cruelly spurns Violetta. When he learns the truth, it is too late because she is mortally ill with tuberculosis. The tender opening chords on the strings and the lovely but deeply sad melody (still on violins and cellos) of this prelude sum up the heartbreaking story.

FADED BEAUTY

The inspiration for Dumas's play *La Dame aux Camélias*, on which *La Traviata* is based, was the celebrated courtesan Marie Duplessis, who died in 1847 from tuberculosis at the age of just twenty-three. According to Dumas, Marie acquired her name because she presented prospective lovers with a camelia, adding: "Come and see me when it fades." And since camelias fade quickly, her message was clear!

A SENSE OF DRAMA

Giuseppe Verdi's long and illustrious career throughout the 19th century coincided with Italy's victorious struggle for political unity and independence. Many of his operas echoed this patriotic movement, making him into a national hero. From a broader musical standpoint, Verdi combined the Italian operatic tradition of *bel canto*, or "beautiful singing," with a powerful sense of drama. According to some, he was the greatest of all operatic composers. *La Traviata*, which he composed during the middle years of his life, is one of his best-loved works.

The Villa Santa Agata, where Verdi (left) spent most of his later years.

MAN OF THE PEOPLE

Verdi came from a humble peasant background, and in many ways he remained a man of the people all his life. When he became rich, he bought a fine country estate, but he still enjoyed sharing in the daily work of exercising the horses and tending the crops. Toward the end of his life, he became something of a philanthropist and built a small hospital near his estate. He also built a rest home *(left)* near Milan, specifically for the care of retired and impoverished musicians.

CARL MARIA VON WEBER
1786–1826

Oberon

OVERTURE

Carl Maria von Weber's opera *Oberon*, a tale of medieval romance and magic, concerns a wager between Oberon, King of the Fairies, and his Queen, Titania. As a result of the wager, the knightly Sir Huon of Bordeaux and Reiza, the beautiful daughter of the Caliph of Baghdad, have to undergo a series of tribulations—including a shipwreck, piracy, and slavery—in order to prove their enduring love for each other. Eventually, the two are rescued by a magic horn, which Oberon has given to Sir Huon. Weber's overture instantly casts a magic spell of its own, with a soft horn call, little phrases dancing on flutes and clarinets, and an enchanting cello theme.

FINAL FLOURISH

Oberon, commissioned by the Royal Opera House in London, was Weber's last opera and may have proved too much for him. Already a sick man, Weber traveled from Germany to London to compose the score and supervise rehearsals. The premiere, which Weber himself conducted, was, in his own words, "the greatest success of my life." But within two months he was dead. He was buried in London, but fellow composer Richard Wagner later raised the money to have his remains taken back to Germany.

Above: *A lithograph of Weber's characteristically extravagant conducting gestures.*

SHOWPIECE

The overture to *Oberon*, the original playbill for which is shown (*left*), is heard much more often than the rest of the opera. It is an orchestral showpiece, both in terms of the organization of the music and in the clear way Weber makes the orchestra ring with sound. His imaginative use of the instruments makes him one of the true pioneers of Romantic orchestral music.

KEY NOTES

As a young man, Weber was a dashing and romantic figure who had a reputation for getting in trouble. He was also a beautiful singer · until an accidental drink of nitric acid damaged his voice.

RALPH VAUGHAN WILLIAMS
1872–1958

The Wasps

OVERTURE

The overture to *The Wasps* is part of a suite of incidental music composed for a 5th-century B.C. Greek play. The author, Aristophanes, wrote his comedy as a satire on the political environment in his native Athens. In the play, he made fun of his enemy, Cleon, by bringing Cleon's supporters on stage dressed as wasps. The wasps were armed with stings to torment people who disagreed with them. Vaughan Williams begins his overture, appropriately enough, with a menacing buzz on the strings. The wasps soon vanish and the mood brightens. There is a carefree tune in the style of a folk song or dance, and finally a rhapsodic melody, which is both serene and pastoral in sound.

FRENCH POLISH

Although Vaughan Williams was already an accomplished composer, at age thirty-six he visited Paris to take lessons in orchestration from the French composer Maurice Ravel. As Vaughan Williams himself stated, he wanted to give his music "a little more French polish." One of the first and happiest fruits of these lessons was his overture to *The Wasps*.

TOWN AND COUNTRY

Ralph Vaughan Williams was born in Gloucestershire, in the heart of the English countryside, and many of his compositions seem to breathe the very mood of rural England. Other works of his are inspired by the rich tradition of English church music. However, Vaughan Williams was no musical hermit who was interested only in his own backyard.

He was open to and interested in the musical world around him, which influenced his work. For instance, his nine big symphonies and other concert works reflect his worldly interests.

Vaughan Williams served as an ambulance driver in World War I.

INCIDENTAL MUSIC

Vaughan Williams studied at Cambridge University *(left)*. Some years later, the University theater group decided to stage a production of *The Wasps* by Aristophanes *(far left)* and they invited the composer back to write the incidental music. As it turned out, the production only ran one night, but his splendid overture has been delighting concert-goers ever since.

COUNTRY COLLECTION

Many composers in the early years of the 20th century were afraid that as life became industrialized and more people moved from farms and villages to the big cities, their age-old heritage of folk songs and dances would be forgotten and lost forever. This was what prompted Vaughan Williams to travel about the English countryside, noting down songs and dances wherever he heard them. He collected hundreds of such tunes and arranged the best of them for orchestra. But Vaughan Williams also wrote many new tunes, inspired by his experiences. Some were such clever imitations that people mistook them for traditional folk songs.

Above: *An example of the the traditional folk dancing and singing that gave Vaughan Williams so much pleasure.*

MOVIE MUSIC

Another of Vaughan Williams's musical interests was the cinema, and he wrote the scores for two World War II movies, *49th Parallel* and *Coastal Command*. After

the war, he composed the music for the classic British movie *Scott of the Antarctic (left)*. This was such a success that he later turned it into a symphony, his *Sinfonia Antartica*.

KEY NOTES

Vaughan Williams was not the only famous composer to fight for his country in World War I. Two others were the Frenchman Maurice Ravel and the avant-garde German composer Arnold Schoenberg.

Samuel Ramey and Gianna Rolandi as Figaro and Susanna, two of opera's most engaging lovers.

WOLFGANG AMADEUS MOZART *1756–1791*

The Marriage of Figaro

OVERTURE

Until Mozart's time, overtures were designed, for the most part, to alert the audience that the show was about to start. From the very first note, this famous overture grabs the attention of the audience with its air of excitement and bustle. And typical of Mozart's style, it also bubbles over with tuneful high spirits.

LOVE ON THE RUN

The Marriage of Figaro has a lighthearted plot regarding amorous intrigues. The man who wrote the words to Mozart's triumph was Italian poet Lorenzo da Ponte, who was actually also ordained as a priest. After working with Mozart in Vienna, da Ponte moved on to London and then finally to New York.

KEY NOTES

Analysis of Mozart's papers and inks has shown that he did not compose Figaro *from beginning to end, but according to the type of scene: First the playful, undramatic ones; then the comic, dramatic; then the action scenes; and then the lyrical arias.*

RICHARD WAGNER *1813–1883*

The Mastersingers of Nuremberg

OVERTURE

*T*he *Mastersingers* takes place in 16th-century Nuremberg, Germany, which at the time was one of the most prosperous and cultured cities in Europe. The action revolves around a song contest. In those days, much singing and song involved the weaving of different melodies into complex tapestries of sound. Here, Wagner does the same with the themes from his opera, often running two or three melodies at the same time and then knitting them together into what is known musically as a "symphonic poem." From the first great opening chord to the last, the effect is one of richness, drama, and power.

AT A LOW EBB

Richard Wagner, the undisputed master of German grand opera, was in his late forties when he began work on *The Mastersingers*. At the time, his life was at a low point. He was separated from his first wife, Minna, had no home of his own, and was hopelessly in debt due to his extravagant lifestyle. He even had stopped work on his projected cycle of four gigantic music dramas called *The Ring of the Nibelungs* because he saw no hope of them ever being staged. And yet, in spite of all this, *The Mastersingers* is one of the most joyous and life-enhancing operas that has ever been written.

WAGNER'S INSPIRATION

In the Middle Ages, Nuremberg stood at the crossroads of the main trade routes between Asia and the Atlantic Ocean and between the Mediterranean Sea and northern Europe, making it a cultural center. Its guilds of artists and craftsmen held grand contests of poetry and song and came to be known as "Mastersingers." This was Wagner's inspiration for his opera. Its hero, the shoemaker Hans Sachs, is based on a real-life craftsman, poet, and musician of the time *(right)* who wrote several thousand songs and hundreds of plays and tales.

FAITH IN HIS GENIUS

With *The Mastersingers of Nuremberg*, Wagner's belief that he was destined for greatness was justified. It was largely thanks to King Ludwig II of Bavaria that Wagner was able to stage the operas *The Mastersingers* and *Tristan and Isolde* and to finish his colossal *Ring* cycle. He was summoned by the young king, who loved some of his earlier operas, and appointed royal director of music in Munich. Ludwig even showered him with money and gifts.

LIVING THE GOOD LIFE

Wagner was the exact opposite of the popular image of the artist starving in his garret. Wagner craved the good and the beautiful things of life: fine food and wines, the best clothes, and richly furnished apartments both to live and to work in. He claimed he could not work unless he was surrounded by such luxuries. He even sprayed his rooms with perfume to inspire him!

King Ludwig II (above) and his castle in the Bavarian mountains (left).

KEY NOTES

Another character in The Mastersingers *is Sixtus Beckmesser, a stupid and fussy town clerk. He was Wagner's way of getting back at a famous music critic, Eduard Hanslick, who had attacked his work!*

PYOTR TCHAIKOVSKY
1840–1893

The Nutcracker
MINIATURE OVERTURE

*I*n the ballet *The Nutcracker*, a little girl dreams that the strange, old nutcracker she has been given as a Christmas present turns into a handsome prince, who then transports her to a fabulous kingdom of games and toys and delicious things to eat. The suite, or collection of dances, that Tchaikovsky made from the full ballet score is introduced by this miniature overture. Its nimble rhythms and tunes sparkle like sugar frosting—the perfect prelude to such a world of innocent make-believe.

BEST-LOVED BALLET

Tchaikovsky's *The Nutcracker* is probably the best known and best loved of all ballets, but the composer himself had a low opinion of it. In fact, he only put together his concert suite from the score when another project fell through and he desperately needed a replacement.

RUSSIAN BALLET

For well over a hundred years, Russian dancers, designers, and choreographers (those who plan the movements and steps of a ballet) have been leaders in the world of ballet. But historically, they took their lead from France. Ballet, as we know it, began at the court of the 17th century French King Louis XIV—or the "Sun King" as he was called. It was introduced into Russia by the Tsarina Catherine the Great *(right)* and her Romanov successors, all of whom had great admiration for the French and looked on them as their cultural leaders.

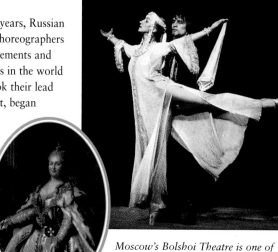

Moscow's Bolshoi Theatre is one of the finest exponents of Russian ballet.

A GREAT ORCHESTRATOR

Tchaikovsky's great strength as a composer was his ability to use the different instruments of the orchestra in much the same way as a painter uses colors—to build up a vivid, multi-layered effect. In *The Nutcracker*, he uses them to create a delicate, magical, almost childlike quality. Elsewhere in his orchestral music, he produces richer, more vibrant sounds. Such brilliant writing for the orchestra followed in the distinguished footsteps of Berlioz, Wagner, and other composers of the Romantic period.

KEY NOTES

The ballet is based on a story, by the German writer E.T.A. Hoffmann, called "The Nutcracker and the King of Mice."

LUDWIG VAN BEETHOVEN *1770–1827*

Fidelio

OVERTURE

This overture introduces the only opera composed by Beethoven. It is a dark tale of tyranny and oppression, set in a state prison in Spain around the beginning of the 17th century. The composer opens with a defiant and forceful tune, echoed by calls on horns and woodwind instruments. The slow introduction is then transformed into a theme that runs right through the overture. Near the end, Beethoven slows the pace again, before launching into a faster ending that brings home the recurring theme in dramatic style.

THE NEW ROMANTIC

Ludwig van Beethoven *(right)* is unique among composers in that he bridged the gap between two of the great ages of music: the Classical age and the Romantic age. In the Classical age of Mozart and Haydn, technique, inventiveness, and order ruled the day. The young Beethoven, too, was a master technician. But as he matured as a composer, the power of his own feelings became steadily more evident and influential in his work. By the time of *Fidelio*, it became clear that Beethoven's dramatic and emotionally based composition had revolutionized the structure of classical music itself. And so began the Romantic age, exemplified by the work of Berlioz, Schumann, and later Brahms.

THE TRIUMPH OF LOVE

The story of *Fidelio* concerns a Spanish nobleman, Florestan, who has been unjustly imprisoned. In the hope of rescuing him, his wife, Leonora, goes to the prison disguised as a boy, Fidelio. In the end, her devotion pays off: Florestan is set free, and the tyrannical prison governor, Don Pizarro, is condemned to the dungeon in his place.

Left: *Florestan and his devoted wife, Leonora, who is seen here dressed as the boy Fidelio.*

REVOLUTIONARY IDEALS

Beethoven lived at the time of the French Revolution. He was an admirer of the young Napoleon Bonaparte *(right)* and was inspired by what he believed was Bonaparte's philosophy. *Fidelio*, a story of justice triumphing over tyranny, is a dramatic expression of these ideals. The reality was somewhat different: Napoleon crowned himself Emperor of France and left the composer feeling profoundly disillusioned.

FOURTH TIME LUCKY

The composition of *Fidelio* (or *Leonora* as it was originally called) did not come easily to Beethoven, and he revised it several times. In the process, he wound up writing three different overtures. The overture known as *Leonora No.3* is as large scale and dramatic in effect as a movement from a symphony, but too weighty to serve as a curtain-raiser. So Beethoven replaced it with this overture, briefer than the others, but much better suited to the purpose.

The Theater an der Wien (left) *was the venue for the premiere of* Fidelio *on November 20, 1805.*

KEY NOTES

Fidelio belongs to a type of opera called "rescue opera," which was very popular during Beethoven's lifetime. An early example was the Belgian composer Grétry's Richard Coeur de Lion ("Richard the Lionheart"), in which King Richard is rescued by his minstrel Blondel. Another is Lodoïska by the Italian-born composer Cherubini, whose work Beethoven much admired.

SIR ARTHUR SULLIVAN *1842–1900*

The Yeomen of the Guard

OVERTURE

The highly successful British partnership of librettist W.S. Gilbert and composer Arthur Sullivan chose the world famous Tower of London as the setting for this much-loved *operetta* (or little opera). In the overture, Sullivan instantly summons up an air of pageantry with a grand and stately march that some people think echoes Wagner's *The Mastersingers*. Sullivan then introduces other, more romantic tunes before rounding off the piece with a return of his proud and noble march.

GUARDING THE TOWER

The Tower of London, dating back to the Norman Conquest of 1066, was a grim prison fortress for centuries. But it has also been the scene of much colorful ceremony. The Yeomen of the Guard, in their scarlet and gold uniforms of the Tudor period, originally formed a royal bodyguard. Popularly known today as "Beefeaters," they remain one of the chief attractions of the Tower.

KEY NOTES

The famous comic operettas of Gilbert and Sullivan are widely known as the "D'Oyly Carte operettas," after the promoter and manager Richard D'Oyly Carte, who brought the two men together.

GIOACHINO ROSSINI *1792–1868*

William Tell

OVERTURE

ioachino Rossini's overture to *William Tell* is as varied and colorful as the opera: A stirring tale of freedom-fighting with a subplot of a love affair. The slow opening section suggests early morning over the Swiss Alps. A storm gathers, breaks with full fury, then dies away again. There is a lovely duet between the cor anglais and the flute. Then comes the trumpet call that announces the arrival of the hero, William Tell, and his fellow patriots. Their breathless gallop is the most famous piece of "hero-to-the-rescue" music ever written and as thrilling a finish as anyone could wish for.

A STORY OF SWISS PATRIOTISM

Central to the story of *William Tell* is Switzerland's fight for independence from Austria. In the opera, the plot is given added spice by a love affair between two of the characters, a Swiss patriot, Arnold, and the daughter of the Austrian governor, Mathilde.

PRODIGIOUS EFFORT

The Italian composer Gioachino Rossini wrote nearly forty operas in less then twenty-five years. This prodigious effort made him both rich and famous, but it also left him utterly exhausted. After *William Tell*, which was his last and grandest opera, he went into semi-retirement and settled in Paris, where he enjoyed the company of a wide circle of friends and admirers. But Rossini could not stop himself from composing completely. A number of charming songs and instrumental pieces, plus two much larger religious works, were produced during this later period of his life.

BON VIVEUR

Rossini had a reputation as a *bon viveur*—someone who enjoys the good things of life, especially food and drink. The much-caricatured composer was certainly something of a gourmet and was credited with inventing several new dishes, including "Tournedos Rossini," made from a steak fillet.

CLEVER COMMENTS

Rossini was a noted wit. One day a young, aspiring composer came to him with two of his own pieces. He played the first one to Rossini and waited for comment. "I prefer the other one," Rossini wickedly declared. And the first time Rossini heard Berlioz's revolutionary new *Symphony Fantastique*, he exclaimed: "Thank God it isn't music!"

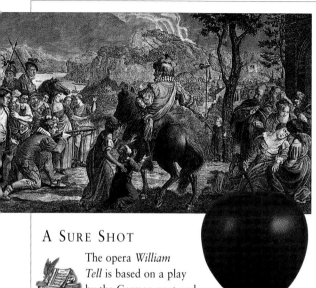

A SURE SHOT

The opera *William Tell* is based on a play by the German poet and dramatist Friedrich Schiller (1759-1805). The hero of the title is a 14th-century Swiss patriot who led his country's fight for freedom from Austria. Both the play and the opera include the famous episode in which the sadistic

Tell's successful shooting of an apple from his son's head confirmed his place as a Swiss national hero.

Austrian governor, Gessler, forces Tell to shoot with his crossbow at an apple placed on his young son's head. Tell succeeds, to the jubilation of his fellow citizens, and later shoots Gessler himself.

BIG IS BEST

Paris in the 19th century boasted some of the biggest and best-equipped theaters and opera houses in Europe. Rossini was one of a number of foreign composers who wrote operas especially for the Paris stage. For instance, his comic opera *Le Comte Ory* (set in the time of the Crusades) was first produced there in 1828. *William Tell* (or, in French, *Guillaume Tell*) followed one year later.

KEY NOTES

A somewhat gentler example of Rossini's legendary wit is the name that he gave to a series of pieces composed toward the end of his life, inspired by his experiences. He called them, "The sins of my old age."

Credits & Acknowledgments

PICTURE CREDITS

Cover /Title and Contents Pages/ IBC: Performing Arts Library/Clive Barda

AKG London: 4(b), 6, 21(bl); Bridgeman Art Library, London/Christie's, London: 8; Hermitage, St.Petersburg: 18(c); Giraudon: 21(r); British Library: 21(cl); Corbis-Bettmann: 5(l); James Davis Travel Photography: 16(bl), 23; ET Archive: 17; Ronald Grant Archive: 5(tr & cr), 12(b); Robert Harding Picture Library/Adina Tovy: 14; David Jacobs: 22; Hulton Getty: 7(tr), 11(bl & cl) 15(r); Images Colour Library: 12(t); Lebrecht Collection: 3 (l & r), 7(c), 9(c), 11(tr), 15(l), 16(cl & tr), 20(r), 24(l); Private Collection: 2; Celene Rosen: 7(bl); NHPA/Stephen Dalton: 10; Performing Arts Library/Clive Barda: 18(r), 20(l); Ron Scherl: 13; Photostage/Donald Cooper: 4(t), 19; Royal College of Music: 9(tr), 24(r); Royal Opera House Archives: 9(bl); Tony Stone Images: 25(c).

All illustrations and symbols: John See